THE CALIFORNIA GOLD RUSH AND THE '49ERS

by Jean F. Blashfield

CAPSTONE PRESS
a capstone imprint

Fact Finder Books are published by Capstone Press,
1710 Roe Crest Drive, North Mankato, Minnesota 56003
www.mycapstone.com

Library of Congress Cataloging-in-Publication Data
Names: Blashfield, Jean F., author.
Title: The California Gold Rush and the '49ers / by Jean F. Blashfield.
Description: North Mankato, Minnesota : Capstone Press, [2017] | Series: Fact
   finders. Landmarks in U.S. history | Includes index. | Includes
   bibliographical references and index. | Audience: Grades 4–6. | Audience:
   Ages 8–10.
Identifiers: LCCN 2017003798 (print) | LCCN 2017004630 (eBook PDF) | ISBN
   9781515771166 (library hardcover) | ISBN 9781515771395 (paperback) | ISBN
   9781515771432 (eBook PDF)
Subjects: LCSH: California—Gold discoveries—Juvenile literature. |
   California—History—1846–1850—Juvenile literature. | Frontier and
   pioneer life—California—Juvenile literature.
Classification: LCC F865 .B64 2017 (print) | LCC F865 (eBook PDF) | DDC
   979.4/04—dc23
LC record available at https://lccn.loc.gov/2017003798

Editorial Credits
Bradley Cole and Gena Chester, editors; Sarah Bennett and Brent Slingsby, designers;
Pam Mitsakos, media researcher; Steve Walker, production specialist

Photo Credits
Getty Images: Bettmann, 21, Underwood Archives, 22 bottom; Newscom: Everett Collection, 25, World History Archive, 10–11; North Wind Picture Archives, 9, 14–15, 17, 18–19; Shutterstock: Africa Studio, 26, Everett Historical, cover, 1, 7, 8, 16, NatalieJean, 28, optimarc, 13, Sean Pavone, 27, trubach, 6 bottom left, Vastram, 23 top middle; The Image Works/©ullstein bild, 23 bottom middle; XNR Productions: XNR/Map, 5

Design Elements:
Shutterstock: Andrey_Kuzmin, ilolab, Jacob J. Rodriguez-Call, Jessie Eldora Robertson, Olga Rutko

Printed and bound in the USA
010399F17

TABLE OF CONTENTS

CLAIMS TO CALIFORNIA

The United States was growing fast in the 1840s. Thousands of people had begun traveling west along the Oregon Trail. A group turned south, away from the popular Oregon Trail in 1844. They trekked over a peak in the Sierra Nevada and into the Sacramento Valley. This was the opening of the California Trail.

Deadly Journey

The timing of journeys to the West was important. One party departing from Illinois was led by George and Jacob Donner. They started their route in April 1846, dangerously late in the season.

The Donner Party took a shortcut through the Wasatch Mountains. However, this path had not been tested and ended up causing the group to fall behind schedule. By the time they reached the pass through the Sierra Nevada, it was snowing. They were stuck. The party of 82 travelers built makeshift shelters to keep from freezing, but they ran out of food. They were forced to turn to **cannibalism** in order to survive.

Only 47 people survived. They were finally rescued in early 1847. Today that pass is called Donner Pass.

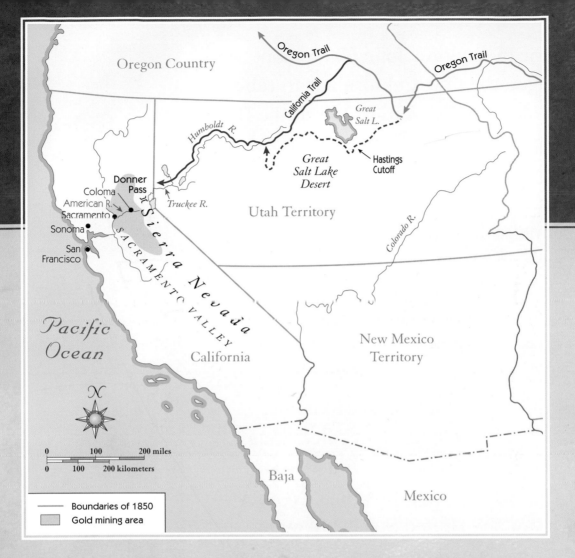

Despite the difficult **terrain** and challenging winter weather, many settlers managed to reach California. However, about 10,000 Mexican ranchers and their employees already lived there. Along with winning its independence from Spain in 1821, Mexico also won Spain's North American colonies. This included Texas, New Mexico, Arizona, and California.

....

terrain—the surface of the land
cannibalism—the practice of eating the flesh of another person

American explorer John C. Frémont encouraged the new Californians to **rebel** against Mexico. The settlers raised the Bear Flag over Sonoma in the Sacramento Valley, claiming California as an independent republic. The Bear Flag Revolt lasted only from June to July 1846. U.S. military soon arrived in the territory to start the Mexican-American War (1846–1848). War broke out between the United States and Mexico in 1846.

Mexico lost the war in 1848. U.S. soldiers raised the American flag at Monterey, claiming California for the United States. Mexico agreed to give the United States all of California except the Baja. Neither Mexico nor the United States knew that gold had just been discovered in California.

DID YOU KNOW?
California's state flag still says California Republic and has a bear on it.

CALIFORNIA REPUBLIC

artwork of a Mexican-American War battle

2

THE DISCOVERY OF GOLD

Captain John Sutter was a Swiss settler in California's Sacramento Valley. He owned a lot of land. In 1848 he hired carpenter James Marshall to help build a sawmill at Coloma. The new sawmill was a small outpost on the south fork of the American River.

John Sutter

John Sutter

After a series of business failures and debt, John Sutter left Germany for America in 1834. Sutter did a lot of traveling. He moved from St. Louis, Missouri, to Santa Fe, New Mexico, and then to the Oregon Territory. He made it all the way to Hawaii before eventually settling in California in 1839.

Sutter quickly worked to establish himself and obtain land in California, which was at the time owned by Mexico. After becoming a Mexican citizen, he was allowed to build his **homestead**. Sutter and the American Indians he befriended worked together to build a settlement. Sutter called his place New Helvetia or "New Switzerland."

Sutter's homestead

While testing the mill wheel, Marshall noticed something sparkly. Among the sand and gravel, he picked out some small, odd-shaped beads of yellow metal. Marshall had Jenny Wimmer, the camp washerwoman and cook, test the beads in **lye**. When the beads did not react to the harsh chemical, Marshall knew he had found gold. It was January 24, 1848.

....

lye—a strong substance used in making soap and detergents
homestead—a piece of land with room for a home and farm

Sutter tried to keep the discovery a secret. Two weeks later Sam Brannan, a San Francisco newspaper and general store owner, found out. Workers from Sutter's mill paid for goods at Brannan's store in gold. After learning of the discovery, Brannan set up another business and loaded up on mining supplies. He travelled to San Francisco, walked through the streets, and shouted, "Gold! Gold!" Brannan knew many people would want to buy his mining supplies to chase his news of gold. He quickly made a fortune selling picks, shovels, and pans to **prospectors**. Within days San Francisco was almost a ghost town. Shopkeepers, blacksmiths, and others had left to find gold on Sutter's land.

prospector—a person who looks for valuable minerals, especially silver and gold

These were the first of about 300,000 people who flocked to the Sierra Nevada mountains. People came from all over the world to strike it rich. Many didn't know how hard the life would be or how few would actually find gold.

DID YOU KNOW?
Sam Brannan founded San Francisco's first newspaper. It was called the *California Star*.

San Francisco during the 1800s

DRAWN BY GOLD

3

After Brannan broke the news, most men from San Francisco left the city in hopes of finding their fortunes. They searched near where Sutter had found gold at the American River. As the news spread across the United States, several thousand more men came to the Sierra Nevada that year.

Fortune hunters began to arrive by January 1849. They came from all over the world, including England, Australia, Peru, and China. Those who arrived that year were called '49ers. These newcomers were counted in the 1850 U.S. **census**. The increased number of residents was enough to make California an official state. California was admitted to the United States on September 9, 1850.

Most working people made less than a dollar a day. But in the California goldfields, 1 ounce (31 grams) of gold could bring $15. People left jobs and school to travel west. Some men brought their families, but most went alone.

Pure gold is so soft it can be shaped by hand.

Fortune hunters went by sea and by land. By land it was about 3,000 miles (4,827 km) from the East Coast to California. Most people traveled by wagon along the Oregon Trail. They joined Missouri settlers heading for Oregon in Wyoming. From there the gold seekers headed south across the Sierra Nevada to the Sacramento Valley.

DID YOU KNOW?
By sea the journey from the East Coast of the United States to California was 18,000 miles (28,962 kilometers). On average it took six months to sail down and around Cape Horn in South America.

census—an official count of all the people living in a country or district

In 1849, no laws existed as to who had the right to claim the land where gold was discovered. Prospectors lived in camps, which came with their own set of rules. Usually a man could claim only as much land along a river as he could dig. This was sometimes no more than 100 square feet (9 square meters).

To stake a **claim**, a prospector pounded wooden stakes into the ground to mark his area. If the claim turned out to have no gold, he would just "pull up stakes" and move on.

Soon there were too many prospectors for the amount of land that might have gold. This forced newcomers to buy claims. To trick people into buying land that had no gold or had already been mined, some sellers planted gold on their claims.

claim—a piece of land given to or taken by someone in order to be mined

Gold seekers were more interested in digging for gold than in living well. One man from Boston, Massachusetts, described the life this way: "I pitched my tent, built a stone chimney at one end, made [a] mattress of fir [branches], and thought myself well fixed for the winter."

Many arrived without giving any thought to how or what they were going to eat. Some men starved rather than leaving their claims to get food. Weakened, they couldn't fight off disease, so many died.

"The Notorious Jumping Frog of Calaveras County"

One common tale told in mining camps involved a cheating man and a bet made on a frog's ability to jump. In the 1860s writer Samuel Clemens, who had recently begun using the name Mark Twain, heard the tale. He turned it into "The Notorious Jumping Frog of Calaveras County."

In the tale, gambler Jim Smiley bets a stranger $40 that his frog can jump farthest. Smiley had trained his frog, named Dan'l, for months. While Smiley is out catching his opponent a frog, the stranger feeds lead to Dan'l. Smiley soon returns with another frog. When the frogs are put on th e floor, Dan'l doesn't move, while the other frog jumps away. The stranger takes his winnings and leaves. It's not until later that Smiley learns what the stranger has done, but it is too late. Smiley never catches the stranger. The story made Mark Twain famous.

Mark Twain

Many miners liked to gamble after a long day of work.

After a hard day of digging, miners wanted to relax and be entertained. Those who still had money to spend, or had found a few flakes of gold, went to the **saloons**. They could get a drink, sing, chat with women, or tell tales to each other.

saloon—a bar where people can buy and drink alcoholic beverages

The easiest way to find gold was to pan for it. Panning means scooping up sand from a riverbed in a pan and swirling it around. The pans have small holes in the bottom, allowing the lighter material to **sift** out. Gold is heavy and sinks to the bottom of the pan.

Those who had no running water on their claim used pickaxes and shovels to dig into the hillsides, looking for gold. Sometimes prospectors built long, wooden frames called **sluices**. They poured large amounts of gravel and soil through the frames along with lots of water. Again, the gold sank to the bottom.

Eventually, some prospectors joined forces to create hard-rock mines. These mines followed a layer of quartz deep into the mountains. Gold was often found along with quartz.

In hard-rock mining, the **ore** had to be hauled out of the ground. It was crushed in huge machines. These loud machines ran 24 hours a day. It was dangerous work.

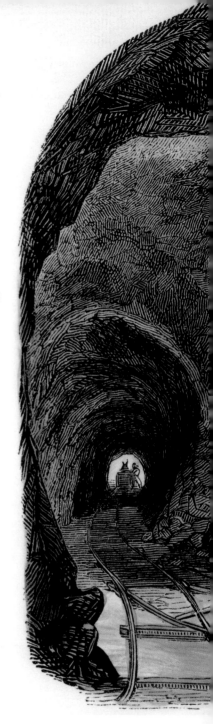

DID YOU KNOW?
A gold vein is also called a **lode**. The Sierra Nevada goldfield was often referred to as the mother lode.

Mining below ground was dangerous work. Miners risked their lives with cave-ins, explosions, toxic fumes, and flooding.

sift—to separate large pieces from small pieces

sluice—a long, slanted trough used to mine gold

ore—a rock that contains metal

lode—a large amount of metal or mineral underground

19

"MINING" THE MINERS

Few prospectors ever found gold. Most of the people who made money during the Gold Rush earned it by selling supplies. They "mined" the miners. At the docks or at the end of the trail, peddlers offered newcomers chances to buy "sure things." They tried to sell newcomers digging sites, space in rooming houses, equipment, food, clothing, or information.

Many people mined for only a few weeks before giving up. Panning and digging were hard, dirty jobs. Discouragement set in easily. Some miners fell prey to criminals, and others got sick and died. Diseases were widespread in the camps. A disease called cholera, spread by **contaminated** water, killed many people. Those who survived often looked for other ways to make a living.

contaminated—dirty or unfit for use

Basic mining tools included a pan, pick axe, and shovel.

The people who sold supplies to the miners helped build California. They constructed houses, grew food, provided entertainment, opened schools and churches — and buried the dead.

One person who made his money supplying the miners was Levi Strauss. He was a Jewish peddler from Germany. He started out selling canvas for tents. Then he hired a seamstress to sew pants for miners who had to kneel on rock all day. He had immediate success. Strauss soon switched from a canvas fabric to a tough cotton cloth called denim. He dyed the material a deep blue, supported the seams of the pants with copper clips, and called the new pants Levi's. His company continues to sell jeans today.

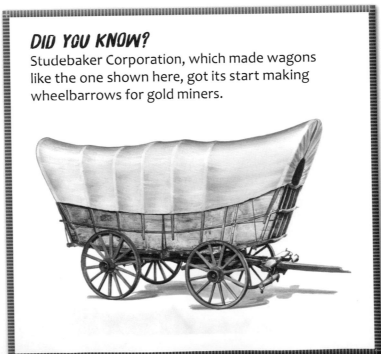

DID YOU KNOW?
Studebaker Corporation, which made wagons like the one shown here, got its start making wheelbarrows for gold miners.

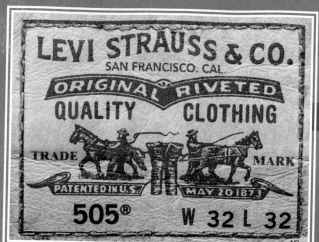

brand patch on Levi's jeans

miners wearing Levi's

WOMEN OF THE GOLD RUSH

About 98 percent of the people who were lured to California during the Gold Rush were men. The few women who took part were often entertainers or saloon keepers. Some worked in the camps as cooks and washerwomen.

Part of the attraction of the Gold Rush for women was that they could earn their own money. That was an important part of the state's **constitution**. California allowed women to keep their own property and money when they married. This was a right unheard of in the other states.

One of the most famous women of the Gold Rush was an African American named Mary Ellen Pleasant. Born a slave, she went to school in Boston and inherited money from her first husband. She and her second husband moved to San Francisco in 1849. There she used her money to open a **boardinghouse**.

Mary Ellen Pleasant

Pleasant may also have lent out money — and gained **interest** on it. She used her wealth to help African Americans in the community. Today she is known as a founder of **civil rights** laws in California.

constitution—the written system of laws that state the rights of the people and the powers of the government

boardinghouse—a lodging house at which meals are provided

interest—the cost of borrowing money

civil rights—the rights that all people have to freedom and equal treatment under the law

THE CHANGES TO CALIFORNIA

More than $500 million in gold had been mined by 1860. Today that is worth about $10 billion. Of the people who actually found gold, few managed to hang onto it. But some were lucky.

The biggest effect of the Gold Rush was the new state's exploding population of various nationalities. California became — and continues to be — a place of great **diversity**.

COST OF 1 OUNCE (28 GRAMS) PURE GOLD DUST
- in 1852, $16
- in 2017, around $1,200

AMOUNT OF U.S. GOVERNMENT'S GOLD RESERVE
- in 1852, $250 million
- in 2015, over $383 billion

modern-day San Francisco

San Francisco, originally the Mexican village of Yerba Buena, was many miles away from the gold mines. But it became the central city of the Gold Rush and the entire West. Theaters there featured singers, dancers, and actors from the East. These performers often went to the camps to entertain.

Writers also flourished during the Gold Rush. Many newspapers were published. Western writer Bret Harte's stories "The Luck of Roaring Camp" and "The Outcasts of Poker Flat" were both set during the Gold Rush.

diversity—variety

27

Some of the effects of the Gold Rush were not good. The environment suffered greatly. Rivers were polluted. Land was dug up, mining chemicals were dumped, and the soil previously used for farmland was destroyed. In many places the destruction caused by the Gold Rush can still be seen.

DID YOU KNOW?
Miners used mercury to pan for gold. Today, traces of mercury **pollute** the gravel and creek beds of more than 40,000 abandoned Californian mines.

Treatment of American Indians was especially bad. About 90 percent of them had already died of diseases brought by the Spanish. When California became a state, the new constitution put the remaining American Indians practically into slavery. Miners were allowed to put them to work in the gold mines without pay. Between 1845 and 1870, the number of American Indians in California dropped from 150,000 to fewer than 30,000.

John Martin, a lawyer for the local Washoe tribe, said, "The miners came, the miners left. We're still trying to clean up the waste they left behind." Many Californians enjoy the idea that their state grew from hardy, independent gold seekers. They like to remember that the '49ers settled their state. But at the same time, Californians remember that their settling of the state changed the lives of American Indians forever.

To this day, Californians are reminded of their Gold Rush **heritage**. California is known as the Golden State. The state flower is the golden poppy, and the state's motto is "Eureka!" meaning "I have found it!"

pollute—to make something dirty or unsafe
heritage—history and traditions handed down from the past

GLOSSARY

boardinghouse (BORD-ing-hows)—a lodging house at which meals are provided

cannibalism (KA-nuh-buhl-izm)—the practice of eating the flesh of another person

census (SEN-suhs)—an official count of all the people living in a country or district

civil rights (SI-vil RYTS)—the rights that all people have to freedom and equal treatment under the law

claim (KLAYM)—a piece of land given to or taken by someone in order to be mined

constitution (kon-stuh-TOO-shuhn)—the written system of laws that state the rights of the people and the powers of the government

contaminated (kuhn-TAM-uh-nay-tid)—dirty or unfit for use

diversity (dye-VUR-si-tee)—variety

heritage (HER-uh-tij)—history and traditions handed down from the past

homestead (HOHM-sted)—a piece of land with room for a home and farm

interest (IN-trist)—the cost of borrowing money

lode (LODE)—a large amount of metal or mineral underground

lye (LYE)—a strong substance used in making soap and detergents

ore (OR)—a rock that contains metal

pollute (puh-LOOT)—to make something dirty or unsafe

prospector (PRAHS-pek-ter)—a person who looks for valuable minerals, especially silver and gold

rebel (ri-BEL)—to struggle against the people in charge of something

saloon (suh-LOON)—a bar where people can buy and drink alcoholic beverages

sift (SIFT)—to separate large pieces from small pieces

sluice (SLOOSS)—a long, slanted trough used to mine gold

terrain (tuh-RAYN)—the surface of the land

CRITICAL THINKING QUESTIONS

1. In what ways were eastern U.S. settlers unprepared for their journey west?

2. If you were a settler living in the eastern half of the United States at the time of the Gold Rush, would you have traveled west in search of gold? Why or why not?

3. Upon reaching California, men quickly made claims and started looking for gold. What is a claim?

READ MORE

Hall, Brianna. *Strike It Rich!: The Story of the California Gold Rush.* Adventures on the American Frontier. North Mankato, Minn.: Capstone Press, 2016.

Levy, Janey. *Life During the Gold Rush.* What You Didn't Know About History. New York: Gareth Stevens Pub., 2013.

Raum, Elizabeth. *The California Gold Rush: An Interactive History Adventure.* Mankato, Minn.: Capstone Press, 2016.

INTERNET SITES

Use Facthound to find Internet sites related to this book.

Visit *www.facthound.com*

Just type in 9781515771166 and go!

Check out projects, games and lots more at
www.capstonekids.com

INDEX